The Switch Witch

Written and Illustrated

by Charity A. O'Neill-O'Kane

Dedicated to Tiernan, my creative kid, who inspired me to write this book so that we could hand it on to his cousins, Collin and Owen.

We'd like to introduce you to the Halloween Witch or as some of us call her, The Switch Witch.

Not everyone is lucky enough to know the Switch Witch. On Halloween night, she visits houses where good children with wonderful imaginations live.

The Switch Witch lives in an old haunted house, that is not your typical haunted house. It does not have ghouls or ghosts to scare you, ... just her black cat named "Magic", her patch of pumpkins and a cornfield.

Mrs. Switch, as her friends and neighbors call her, loves children and loves to play. She is truly a child at heart.

Every Halloween she enjoys seeing children dressed up in costumes. She rides on her broomstick to visit schools and towns to see Halloween parades and trick-or-treaters.

She cackles, because that is how witches laugh, as she enjoys all of their creative costumes. If you are lucky, you can catch a glimpse of her as she glides by the moon.

You might ask, "Why is she called the Switch Witch?"

Well, many years ago, she was great friends with a little boy named Gavin.

Gavin loved Halloween, almost as much as The Switch Witch. He would get dressed up as his favorite character and parade around at school. In the evenings, he would trick-or-treat around his neighborhood and fill his pillowcase with more candy than any other child in town. Then he would go see the Switch Witch and the two of them would enjoy eating their candy together.

However, The Switch Witch always noticed that Gavin became a bit wild and out of control when he ate all of that candy. She also noticed that Gavin's teeth were starting to turn grey and rot from all of the sugar. Sometimes Gavin would even get sick from eating too much candy at one time.

One year, Mrs. Switch decided that she did not want to see her dear friend Gavin get so sick from all the treats. So she came up with a plan.

"Gavin," she said, "this year after you finish your trick-or-treating, I want you to pick your favorite three pieces of candy. Then put the rest into a special spot. Leave it in your sack next to your lit jack-o-lantern. Keep your lantern lit so I know where it is and that you believe in The Switch Witch. Don't worry, I will blow out the candle when I arrive."

"Once you are asleep," she continued, "I will come by on my broomstick and use my magic wand. In the morning you will find a treat that will be much better than candy!"

So Gavin did as the Switch Witch asked. The next morning when Gavin woke up, he ran downstairs to see what happened to his bag of candy.

He was so surprised to find a book! Gavin loves to read and he could read the story over and over. This was much better than a bag of candy that would be gone in a few days. This book would last for years and could be shared with friends and family.

From that point on the Switch Witch visited homes of children who believed in fairy tales and had strong imaginations. The story of the Switch Witch spread as one child told another. She switched their candy into books, toys, art supplies, puppets, etc. that would help them to build their imaginations and creativity.

So if you believe in this tale and in your imagination, we hope that the Switch Witch comes to visit you this Halloween!

Happy Halloween!

Made in the USA
Middletown, DE
09 October 2023

40474298R00020